ITALIA

Milano

Bologna

Firenze

Roma

Sardegna

Napoli

Palermo

For Elsa and Malin

"Trust God, work hard, and dream big!"

—Chaplain Keith

www.mascotbooks.com

For more information, please contact:
Mascot Books
560 Herndon Parkway #120
Herndon, VA 20170
info@mascotbooks.com

Library of Congress Control Number: 2016915811

CPSIA Code: PRT1116A
ISBN-13: 978-1-63177-727-1

Printed in the United States

JOY & FINLEY

THE ITALIAN RACE

by
Rachel and
Keith Ingram
ILLUSTRATED BY
NAZAR HOROKHIVSKYI

Joy, Finley, and Sir Sam are a daring lot.
Wherever there is action or adventure, they are sought!

They join in races, solve mysteries, and explore uncharted lands,
As they learn about cultures and history firsthand.

While traveling through Italy they join in a car race,
And with their car, Espresso, they'll win if they stay on the chase....

Roaring over the cobbles through the town of Pepperoni,
Espresso is the fastest race car from here to Maddaloni!

With Joy, Finley, and Sir Sam at the wheel,
They closed in on the Bolognese brothers with zeal!

"**Brava!**" Finley cheered as the brothers came into sight.
"We can win the race!" Joy said as she cornered right.

As they rounded the corner an
ominous sky filled their view.
Dead ahead were ravioli storm clouds,
and they were starting to spew!

Espresso screeched to a stop as
ravioli rained from the sky.
If the storm had stopped them, then
the brothers had to be nearby.

"Oh no! Pomodoro has crashed!"

Joy said as she spotted their car.
The brothers had wrecked into an olive grove not far.

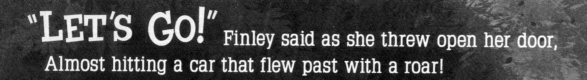

"**LET'S GO!**" Finley said as she threw open her door,
Almost hitting a car that flew past with a roar!

It was mischievous Mezzelune, who raced all alone.
He had lots of race trophies, but none were his own.

"Uh-oh. If he reaches them first..." Joy said unhappily,
"He'll take the golden pizza trophy the brothers won in Napoli!"

"He's going to get there first!" Finley said as they all picked up speed.
The trio arrived just in time to see Mezzelune succeed.

"MWAHA HAHAHA!"

Mezzelune laughed as he jumped into his car.
"Arrivederci, all! I've got another great find for my repertoire!"

Mezzelune zoomed away in a hail of sticky pasta,
As he headed back toward the town of Pepperoni's piazza.

"Cheer up,
Bolognese brothers! We'll get your trophy back," Finley said.

"Andiamo, to Espresso! Adventure is ahead!"

They followed Mezzelune's tracks through the trees,
As the ravioli pasta storm started to ease.

"He's heading back to Pepperoni!" Joy said as they sped for the town.
"We have to beat him to the tunnel if we're going to slow him down."

Pepperoni

Finley looked at her map, found a shortcut, and exclaimed, "Hey!
Take Via Zucchini, it's the fastest way!"

Espresso cornered onto Via Zucchini when the Bolognese brothers objected,
"No, no, no, at the end of Via Zucchini is where all the zucchini are collected!"

"Va bene!" Joy said as they zoomed toward the zucchini pile.
"Espresso has a hidden trick!" she said with a smile.

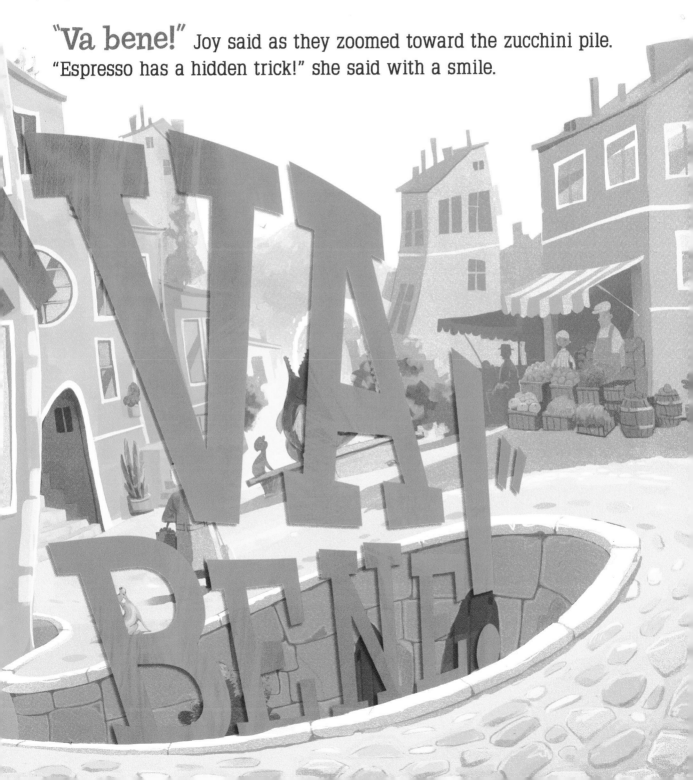

Espresso had fender bender bars from the Napoli race,
Because the sisters knew dents in Napoli were commonplace.

"Deploy the fender bender bars!

Joy said as the pile got closer.
"Deploying now!" Finley said as she kept her composure.

Espresso crashed valiantly through the mountain of zucchini,
While everyone in the car, including Sir Sam, started screaming.

Espresso came to a halt and her wipers cleared their view,
They looked all around to see if Mezzelune made it through.

Much to their surprise, Mezzelune was stopped.
They had blocked his way to the tunnel and his plan had flopped!

Mezzelune started to run as a last escape endeavor.
"Go, Sir Sam! Go!" Finley said, knowing Sir Sam could run forever.

Sir Sam caught Mezzelune and tackled him to the ground.
"Good job, Sir Sam!" Finley said as they gathered around.

Joy helped Mezzelune up while the brothers retrieved their trophy.
"Sorry I took it," Mezzelune said. "I guess I'm just lonely."

At that moment they realized that Mezzelune didn't have any friends,
So he stole things to get some attention instead.

"It's okay," the Bolognese brothers said with an idea.
"Let's all be friends and go eat at a pizzeria!"

"Hooray!" Joy, Finley, and Sir Sam happily cheered,
As everyone's dream of winning the race disappeared.

After all, winning a race shouldn't be the ultimate quest,
But making new friends and having adventures is always the best!

As the new friends chatted and walked toward Espresso,
A race official ran frantically toward the adventurous trio.

"Miss Joy and Miss Finley, a message for you just came!
It says urgent and confidential from M&D!" he proclaimed.

Joy read the letter as Finley and Sir Sam waited with excitement.
"Hmm," Joy said, "we're going to need a pilot."

"Adventure awaits us in a country with history.
Onwards to London, to help solve a mystery!"

JOY & FINLEY THE ITALIAN RACE

Pepperoni: Don't ask for this on your pizza in Italy! You will get peppers, not yummy meat!

Espresso: The type of coffee Italians drink. It's small, very strong, and makes you want to drive fast!

Bolognese: A pasta dish with meat sauce. It's from northern Italy and is a very hearty dish!

Pomodoro: "Tomato" in Italian. Italians love their tomatoes, but traditional Italian spaghetti does not include tomato sauce!

Mezzelune: "Half-moon" in Italian. It is a type of pasta that is half-moon shaped and looks like ravioli!

Napoli: The Italian name for the city of Naples, where pizza was invented!

Arrivederci: "Bye!" in Italian, but it's used when saying "bye" to a grown-up. To say bye to your friends, you would say, "Ciao!"

Piazza: An Italian town square. Every Italian town has a piazza, where Italians gather for fun, business, and food!

Andiamo: "Let's go!" in Italian.

Va Bene: An Italian phrase meaning "it's okay" or "no problem." Italians use it a lot!

Zucchini: Italians grow this type of squash everywhere! It's very yummy and easy to grow. You can make your own giant pile of zucchini in your garden!

Mille Miglia: "Thousand miles" in Italian. The Mille Miglia was an Italian car race from Brescia to Rome and back, during the late 1920s to the 1950s. Today, there is a classic and vintage car version where the drivers follow the old race course, just not as fast!

About the Authors

Keith and Rachel Ingram lived in Naples, Italy, for three years and traveled Europe with their two young daughters. Surprised by the reluctance of other families to travel with their small children, they decided that more kids (and grown-ups) needed to experience the world! Inspired by Rachel's childhood dream to be Indiana Jones and Keith's love of winged and wheeled machines, Joy, Finley, and Sir Sam were created. *Joy & Finley* encourages girls to be anything they want to be, to have worldwide adventures, and to know that sometimes it's the boys who need to be rescued!

www.joyandfinley.com